# Race of the
# RIVER
# RUNNER

### by Geoff Smith
### illustrated by Winson Trang

HOUGHTON MIFFLIN        BOSTON

Sᴜɴ Lɪᴜ followed his father across the busy New York City docks. Horses pulled carts. Workmen carried heavy sacks.

The great steamboat *River Runner* was about to sail up the Hudson River.

Sun's father was heading to Albany on business. At the last minute, he had asked Sun to come along. On board the ship, Sun's father went right to his room to work. But Sun set off to explore.

Sun zipped up the stairs to the very top deck. It was like standing on a mountain. The blue water sparkled in the morning light. Sun wished his father could see how beautiful it was.

5

"What's your name, sailor?" a voice boomed.

Sun turned to see a man smiling right at him.

"I'm Francis Skiddy," said the man, "the pilot of this fine ship. Come on into my house."

"The best thing about life on a steamboat is that everyone is coming from or going to somewhere else," said Captain Skiddy. "What's your story?" His smile glowed like the buttons on his jacket.

Sun explained that he had been born in China. But because of his father's work, his family had moved to London, then Boston, and now New York.

"I don't know where to call home," said Sun.

"I've lived on boats all my life. I'll tell you one thing I've learned," Captain Skiddy said. "Keep your eyes open and remember what you see, and you'll always carry your home with you."

Sun sat on an old, empty apple crate. The big man turned the boat's huge wooden wheel. His hands were hard and red. As he steered, the captain told about life on the river.

Just before lunch another steamboat pulled up next to them.

"It's the *Hudson Queen*!" said Captain Skiddy. Looks like she wants a race. What do you think, Sun?"

"Yes!" cried Sun.

Captain Skiddy sounded the whistle.

"Yell into that pipe," shouted the captain. "Tell the engine room Full Steam Ahead!"

Sun stood on his toes and yelled. The engine began to chug.

Black smoke poured from the stacks of both boats. Orange sparks flew into the air. Huge wakes of water splashed along the shore. People on both boats cheered. The race was on!

As the *River Runner* pulled ahead, people on land stopped to watch. The sight of the two steaming giants fighting it out was too good to miss. A man rode his bicycle along the shore trying to keep up.

The *River Runner's* side wheel chopped the water. But the *Hudson Queen* chugged by her side.

"Rocks ahead!" Captain Skiddy suddenly yelled. "They're trying to get us to stop short! What do you say we do, Sun?"

"More steam!" Sun yelled. Something about Captain Skiddy made him feel brave.

The *River Runner's* engine roared. The rocks lay straight ahead!

At the last moment, the captain spun the wheel. The *River Runner* shot in front of the *Hudson Queen*. The other boat turned into calm waters and slowed.

"I'd say we got her good," Skiddy laughed.

"I'd say so!" Sun cheered.

The *River Runner* pulled up to Albany later that
night. The moon sat fat and bright in the black sky.
As he left the boat, Sun thanked the Captain for a
story that he would always carry with him.